To B. –LS
For my dad, the allergic beekeeper. –RA

About This Book The illustrations for this book were done using rubber stamps, ink, and digital collage. This book was edited by Susan Rich and designed by Rilla Alexander with art direction by David Caplan. The production was supervised by Ruiko Tokunaga, and the production editor was Jen Graham. The text was set in RillAround.

 • Little, Brown and Company • Hachette Book Group • 1290 Avenue of the Americas, New York, NY 10104 • Visit us at LBYR.com • First Edition: April 2019 • Little, Brown and Company is a division of Hachette Book Group, Inc. • The Little, Brown name and logo are trademarks of Hachette Book Group, Inc. • The publisher is not responsible for websites (or their content) that are not owned by the publisher. • Library of Congress Cataloging-in-Publication Data • Names: Snicket, Lemony, author. | Alexander, Rilla, illustrator. • Title: Swarm of bees / by Lemony Snicket ; illustrated by Rilla Alexander. • Description: First edition. | New York : Little, Brown and Company, 2019. | Summary: A horde of bees and a young boy race around town wreaking havoc on the townspeople. • Identifiers: LCCN 2017041812| ISBN 9780316392822 (hardcover) | ISBN • 9780316392792 (ebook) | ISBN 9780316392815 (library edition ebook) • Subjects: | CYAC: Bees—Fiction. • Classification: LCC PZ7.S6795 Sw 2019 | DDC [E]—dc23 • LC record available at https://lccn.loc.gov/2017041812 • ISBNs: 978-0-316-39282-2 (hardcover), 978-0-316-39279-2 (ebook), 978-0-316-52933-4 (ebook), 978-0-316-52934-1 (ebook) • PRINTED IN CHINA • APS • 10 9 8 7 6 5 4 3 2 1

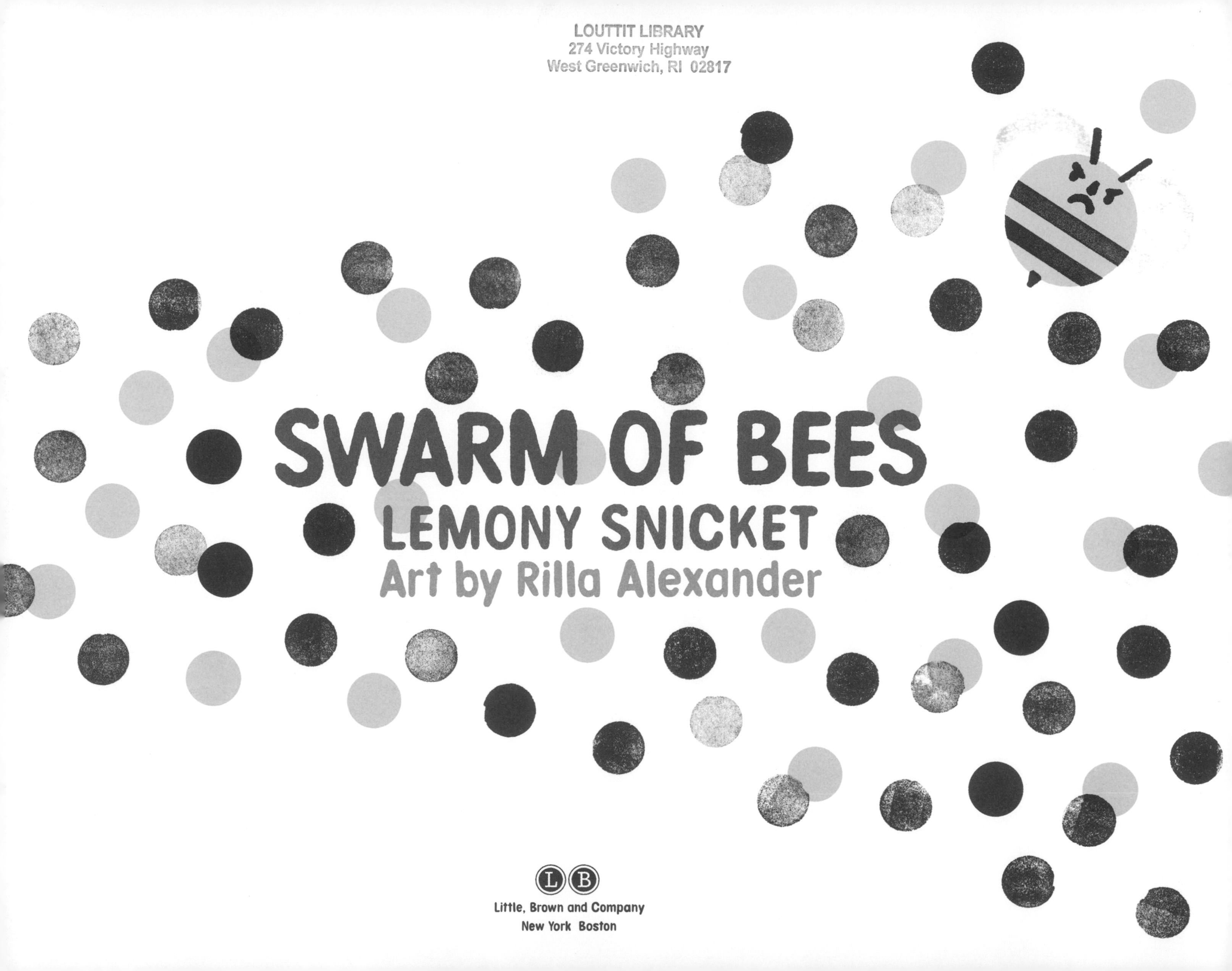

SWARM OF BEES

LEMONY SNICKET

Art by Rilla Alexander

LB
Little, Brown and Company
New York Boston

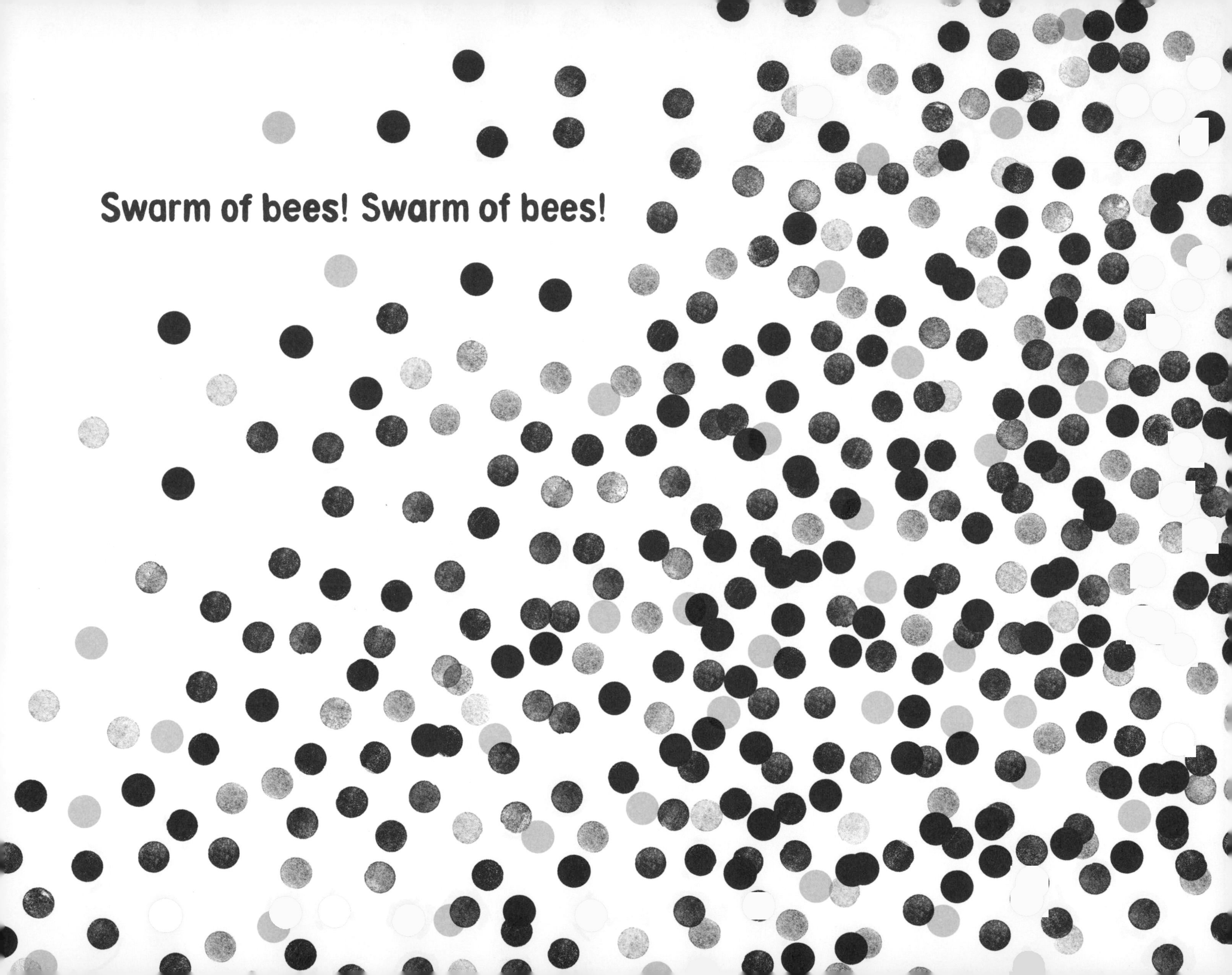

Swarm of bees! Swarm of bees!

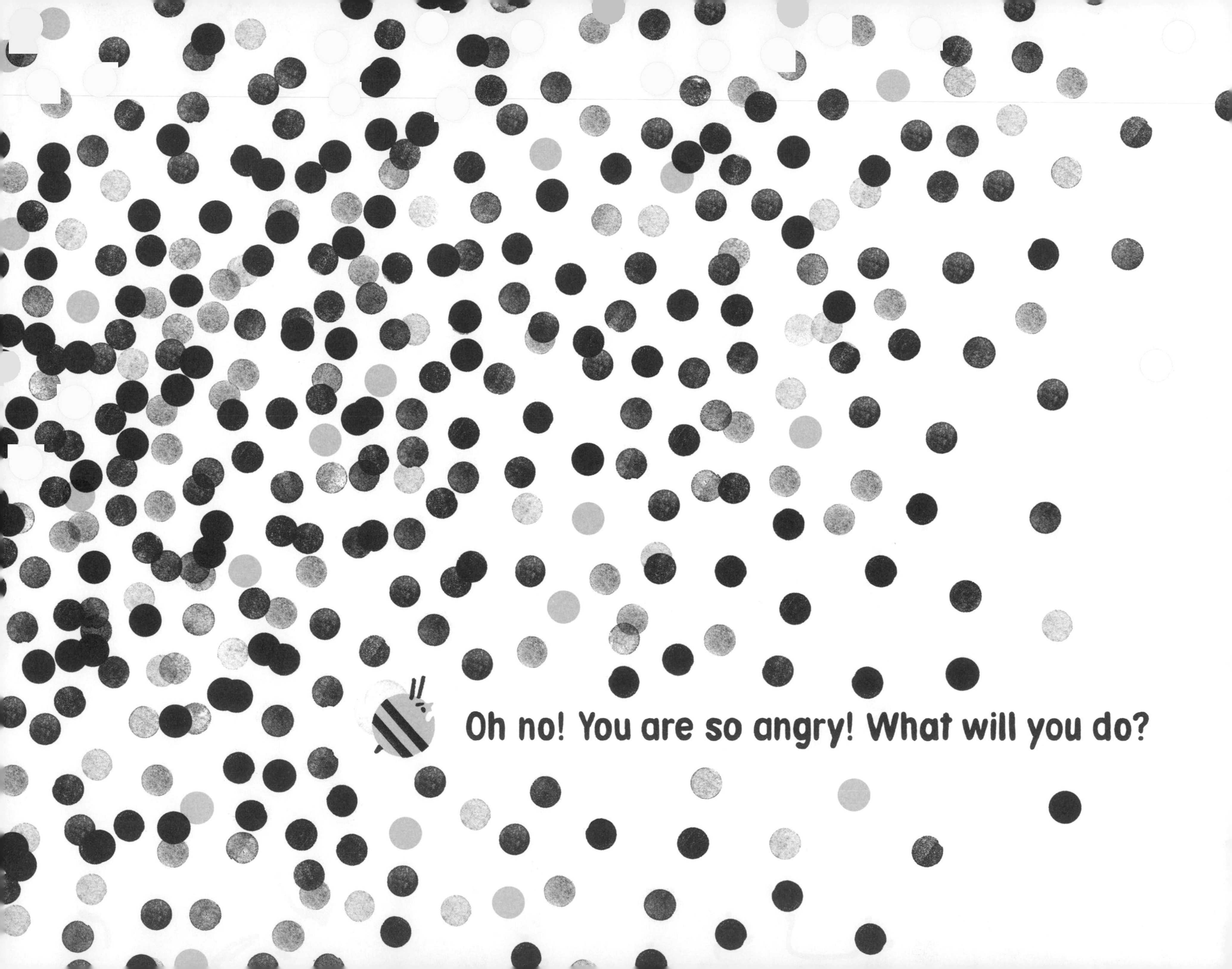

Oh no! You are so angry! What will you do?

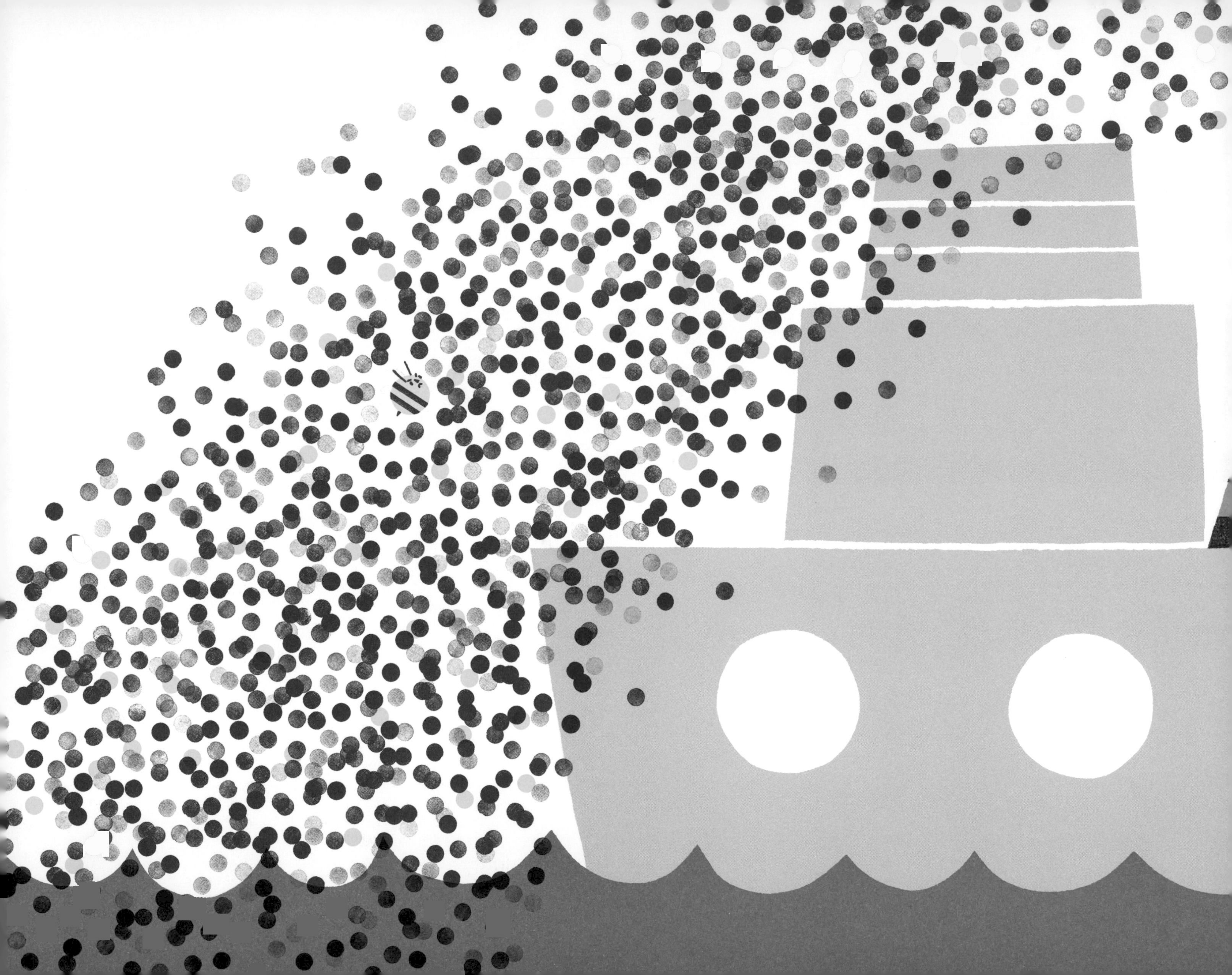

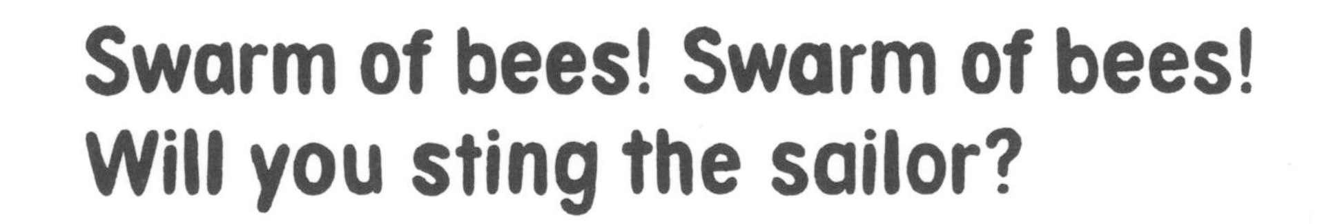

Swarm of bees! Swarm of bees!
Will you sting the sailor?

No! He's been on a ship for nine months and is hurrying to hug his mother.

Swarm of bees! Swarm of bees!
Will you sting the mother?

No! She's about to tell the bricklayer all about her new hairdo.

Swarm of bees! Swarm of bees!
Will you sting the bricklayer?

No! He's starting a new part of the wall.
He is feeling very busy and very hungry.

Swarm of bees! You are still feeling angry!
But you can't sting anyone at the food truck!

The chefs are chopping onions as quick as they can, and the customers are deciding what to drink with their lunches.

You can't sting the cat!
The cat is trying very carefully to hide in the grass.
And, cat, you can't pounce on the bird!
It has a worm in its mouth!

Swarm of bees! Swarm of bees!
You can't sting the man in the second-floor
apartment watching television!

His window is shut, anyway, because his neighbors are making so much noise.

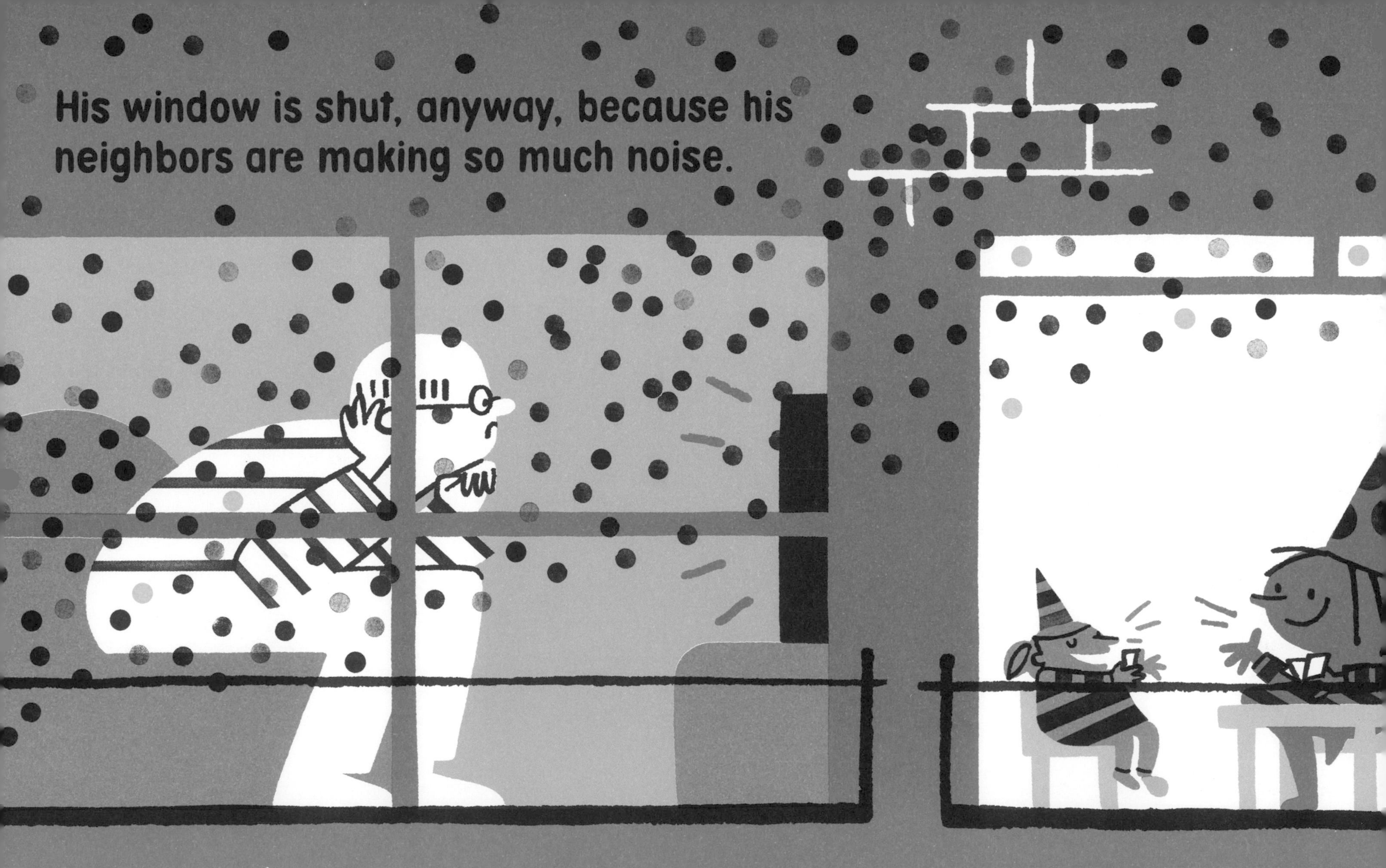

And you can't sting the neighbors! They are playing card games on the balcony and the little cousin is about to win!

You are still angry,
but you can't sting the little cousin!

She already hurt herself today when she stubbed her toe, and that's why she's wearing that bandage.

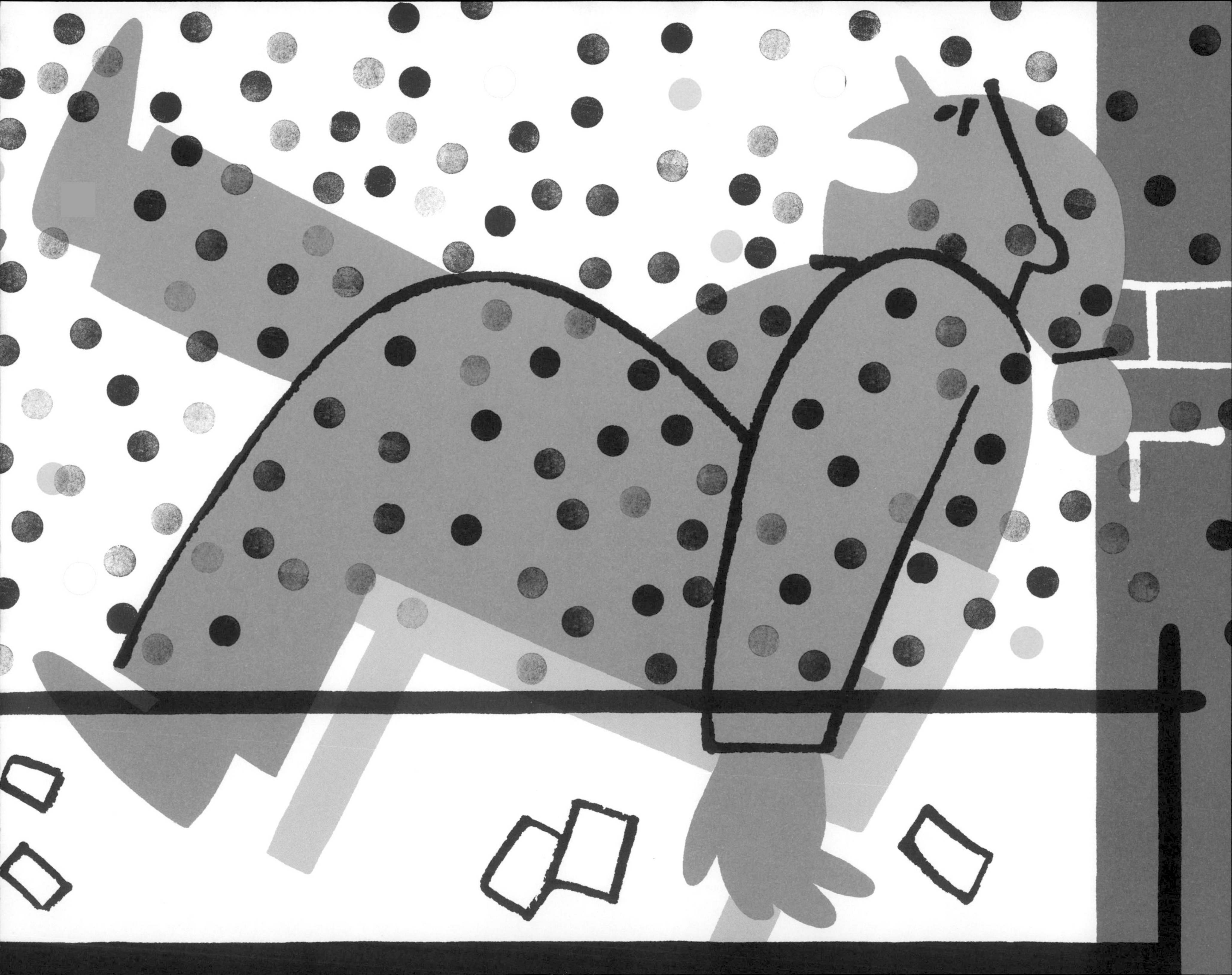

Swarm of bees, are you going to sting
the boy? He keeps throwing tomatoes!
He threw one at the little cousin
and stained her bandage!

He threw one at the neighbor's window and made a mess!

He threw two tomatoes at the cat

and three tomatoes at the bird,

who dropped the worm into
a tomato on the ground!

The boy threw a bunch of tomatoes at the food truck! He shouldn't do that!

The boy threw tomatoes at the bricklayer, and he threw tomatoes at the mother's hairdo, and look! Swarm of bees!

He threw a tomato at the sailor, and the sailor is chasing him!

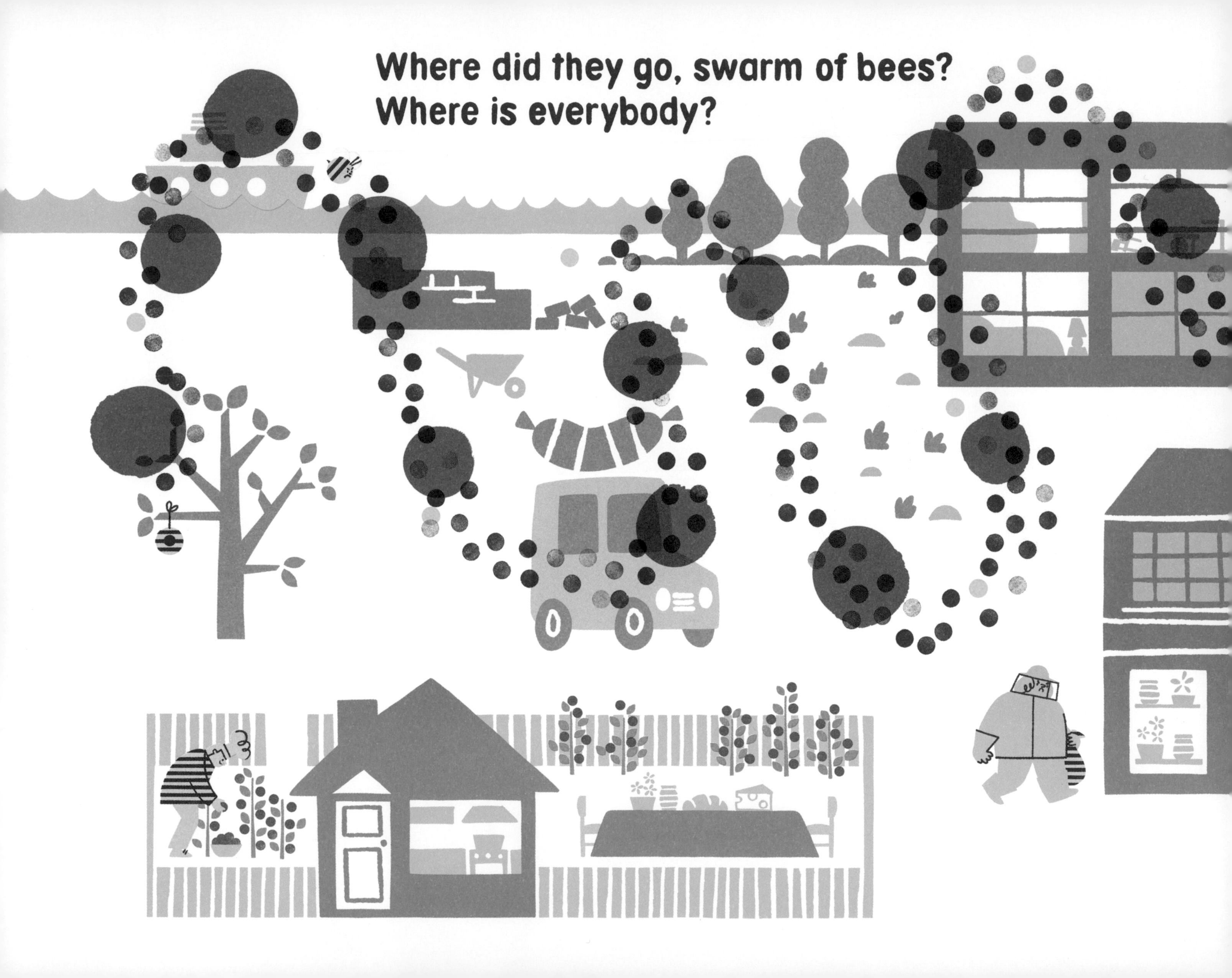

Where did they go, swarm of bees?
Where is everybody?

In the backyard?
Watch out for the laundry!
In the alley?
Watch out for the tow truck!
Around the corner?

Watch out for the beekeeper!

Beekeeper??

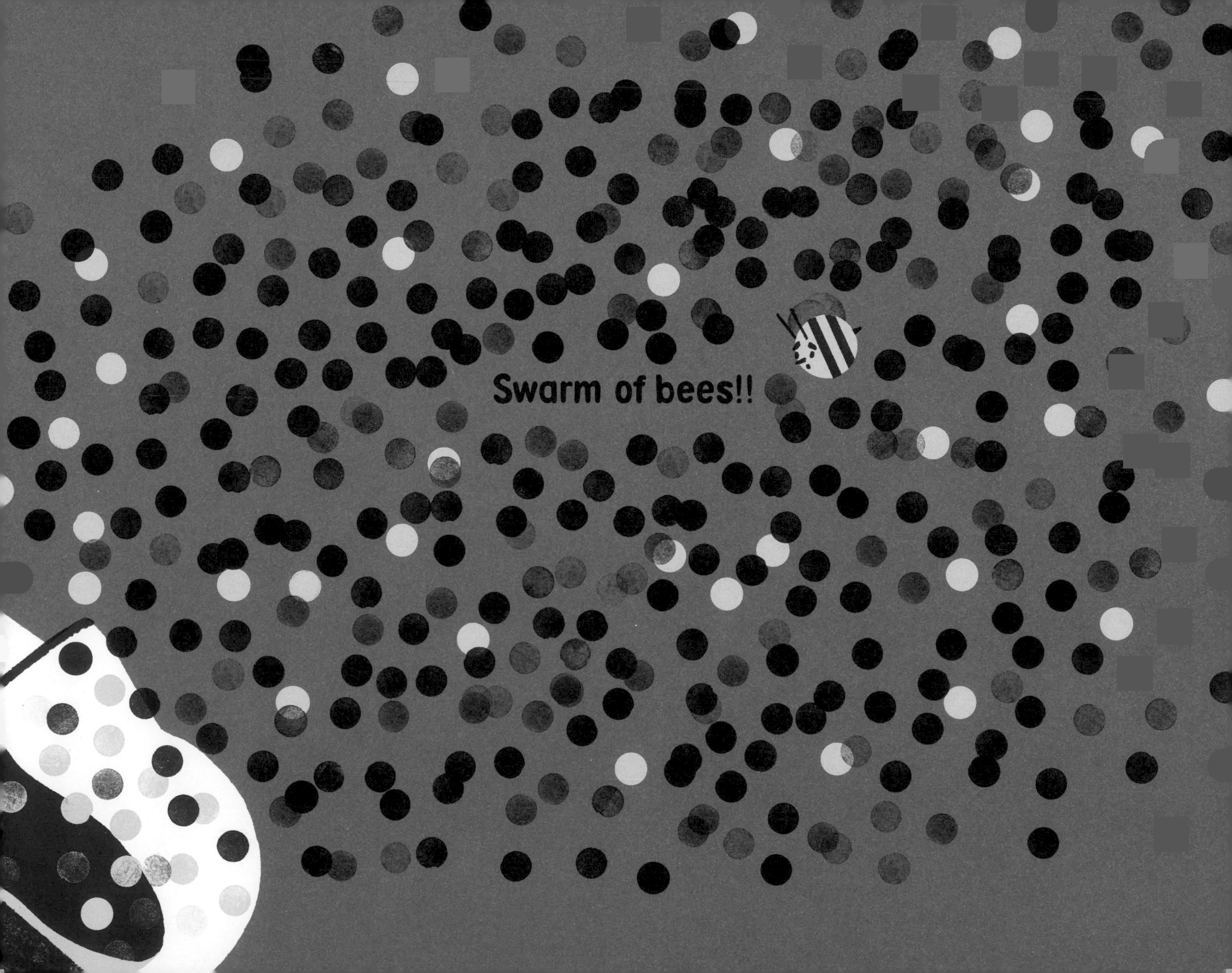
Swarm of bees!!

Well, now you're in a sack.

It's warm and cozy in there.

You calmed down

and soon you'll be going home.

It can feel good to be angry.

It can feel better to stop.

And now...